A

Aphorisms

César Vallejo

Translated from the Spanish
by Stephen Kessler

A Bilingual Edition

GREEN INTEGER
KØBENHAVN & LOS ANGELES
2002

GREEN INTEGER
Edited by Per Bregne
København / Los Angeles
(323) 937-3783 / www.greeninteger.com

First Green Integer Edition 2002
Reprinted in 2020

The contents of this book were first published in the magazine *Universidad de México* in 1992, selected from Vallejo's notebooks by Vicente Quirarte. The translations previously appeared in *Semi-dwarf Quarterly*.

Publication of this book was made possible, in part, through a grant from the Alma White Memorial Fund.

Book Design: Douglas Messerli and Pablo Capra
Cover photograph of César Vallejo

LIBRARY OF CONGRESS CATALOGING-IN-PUBLICATION DATA
Vallejo, César [1892–1938]
Aphorisms
ISBN: 978-1-931243-00-1
p. cm. – Green Integer: 52
I. Title II. Series III. Translator

Green Integer books are published for Douglas Messerli
Printed in the United States of America

Preface

These are not aphorisms in the classical sense of philosophic gemstones cut and polished to epigrammatic perfection. They are more like thoughts-in-progress from the notebooks of a radical modernist poet trying to regain his bearings after a consciousness-shaking encounter with Soviet socialism. Vallejo, one of the most distinctive and challenging individual voices in a period of great creative ferment throughout Europe and especially among poets writing in Spanish, appears to have experienced in 1928 an almost religious conversion to Marxism. From Paris, where he had been self-exiled from his native Peru since 1924, he traveled to both Russia and Spain toward the end of that decade, and the dynamic tension between his own subjective, visionary poetics and a desire for solidarity with the masses both energizes and haunts these writings.

Born in 1892 in a small town in the Andes, Vallejo published his first book of poems, *Los heraldos negros,* in 1919 to critical acclaim. It was followed, in 1922, by *Trilce,* one of the strangest and most astonishing books of poetry ever written; the author was said to have invented surrealism before the Surrealists. Later, in Paris, he dismissed the Surrealists and their dogmatic manifestos as bourgeois esthetes with no connection to the working class. Yet it's clear from his own poetry that he was anything but a propagandist. Some of the essays and criticism he wrote from Paris for Peruvian magazines and newspapers were polemical, but in his later poetry, charged as it is with a passionate affinity for the common man, the creative imagination is wildly inventive, often hallucinatory, intensely compressed with a linguistic eccentricity that only the intellectual vanguard might fully appreciate. This esthetic/ideological dialectic or internal struggle for both political and poetic integrity appears to be what he is working out in the aphorisms.

Vallejo died in Paris in 1938, leaving behind a substantial body of unpublished writing. Read alongside the later poetry (most comprehensively collected in English in *César Vallejo: The Complete Posthumous Poetry,* translated by Clayton Eshleman and José Rubia Barcia, California, 1978), the aphorisms provide background and insight into the mature artist's sociopolitical, literary, and spiritual obsessions. Selected from Vallejo's notebooks by Vicente Quirarte and published in the magazine *Universidad de México* in 1992 in a special issue commemorating the one-hundredth anniversary of the poet's birth, these fragments, jottings, notes, and pungent zingers offer illuminating glimpses into the working mind of a writer considered by many to be one of the greatest and most original voices of twentieth century poetry.

I wish to thank Dr. B. Pokras for introducing me to these texts, originally published in *Universidad de México* magazine, number 495, April 1992. Grateful acknowledgment is also due to Leonard J. Cirino, editor of *Semi-dwarf Quarterly,* where an earlier, slightly abridged version of this translation first appeared. And thanks, finally, to Douglas Messerli, whose idea it was to make this into a book.

Stephen Kessler

Aphorisms

HE visto tres obreros trabajar y hacer un perno; eso es socialismo de la producción. He visto a cuatro compartir una mesa y un pan: eso es socialismo de consumo.

I've seen three workers work to make one bolt; that's socialism of production. I've seen four share one table and a loaf of bread: that's socialism of consumption.

El bolchevismo es el humanismo en acción. Lo mismo puede decirse del revolucionarismo o comunismo, que son humanismos en acción; es decir, la idea y el sentimiento humanista y el ideal humanista, completado por la acción humanista y técnica para que ese ideal se haga carne.

Bolshevism is humanism in action. The same can be said of revolutionism or communism, that they're humanisms in action; that is, the humanist idea and sentiment and the humanist ideal, fulfilled by humanist action and techniques in order that that ideal may be made flesh.

SE le reprocha a Rusia el hacer que sus artistas hagan arte político. Pues bien: Francia daba medallas de oro a los artistas del Salón que se habían distinguido en las trincheras. Alemania, Inglaterra e Italia hicieron idéntico.

RUSSIA is reproached for the fact that its artists make political art. All right then: France gave gold medals to Salon artists who had distinguished themselves in the trenches. Germany, England and Italy did the same.

Los surrealistas y Larrea buscan la liberación del espíritu anterior a la abolición de las condiciones de clase de la burguesía y hasta independientemente de ella.

The surrealists and Larrea seek the spirit's liberation before the abolition of the class conditions of the bourgeoisie and even independent of it.

Los intelectuales son rebeldes, pero no revolucionarios.

INTELLECTUALS are rebels, not revolutionaries.

LA psicología burguesa de un comunista y la psicología comunista de un burgués.

THE bourgeois psychology of a communist and the communist psychology of a bourgeois.

Los intelectuales burgueses protestan de una sableadura a los antiguos combatientes franceses el 6 de febrero y no protestan de las balas contra los obreros del 12 de febrero. ¿Por qué?

Bourgeois intellectuals protest the slaughter of the old French fighters on February 6 but don't protest the shooting of the workers on February 12. How come?

EL colectivismo en Rusia desbarata ciertas formas individuales de la vida, pero, al propio tiempo, origina otras formas individuales. Se come todo el día en Moscú, es decir, *todas no comen* a la misma hora. *Todos no descansan* el mismo día, según el nuevo calendario.

COLLECTIVISM in Russia ruins certain individual life styles, but at the same time it creates other individual styles. Meals are served all day in Moscow, that is, *not everyone eats* at the same time. *Not everyone rests* on the same day, according to the new calendar.

HAY la revolución en literatura (que no es necesariamente revolución en política: Proust, Giraudoux, Morand, Stravinsky, Picasso) y hay la revolución en literatura (que es necesariamente revolución en política: Prokofiev, Barbusse, Diego Rivera). Esta última revolución es de temas y, a veces, va acompañada de técnica. La primera es de ténica y, a veces, va acompañada de temas. En Rusia sólo se tiene en cuenta o, al menos, se prefiere, la revolución temática. En Paris, la revolución técnica.

THERE is revolution in literature (which is not necessarily revolution in politics: Proust, Giraudoux, Morand, Stravinsky, Picasso) and there is revolution in literature (which is necessarily revolution in politics: Prokofiev, Barbusse, Diego Rivera). The latter revolution is thematic and, at times, is accompanied by technique. The former is technical and, at times, is accompanied by themes. In Russia the only thing that counts or, at least, is preferred, is thematic revolution. In Paris, technical revolution.

La política lo penetra todo. Se difunde enormemente. De ahí que los intelectuales se meten en ella y no siguen indiferentes como antes. Porque siempre ha habido injusticia y se ha muerto de hambre el obrero y lo han abaleado. Y nadie dijo nada. Hoy la conciencia política se agranda y se transparenta.

POLITICS penetrates everything. It's vastly dispersed. So intellectuals get involved and don't go along indifferently as before. Because there has always been injustice and the worker has died of hunger and been shot. And nobody said a thing. Today political consciousness is growing larger and clearer.

La piedad y la misericordia de los hombres por los hombres. Si a la hora de la muerte de un hombre, se reuniese la piedad de todos los hombres para no dejarle morir, ese hombre no moriría.

PITY and compassion of people for other people. If at the hour of someone's death everyone else's pity were joined together to keep him from dying, that person wouldn't die.

EL puro y desadaptado que choca con el mundo de las farsas y de las apañucias.

THE pure and poorly adapted one who crashes against the world of fakes and cheats.

LAS dos clases sociales de Moscú buscan algo: la una de noche; la otra de día.

Both social classes in Moscow are looking for something: one by night, the other by day.

Los bandidos religiosos, al ser regenerados, devienen todos sin dios.

Religious bandits, once converted, all become godless.

Para las almas de absoluto, la muerte es una desgracia intemporal, una desgracia vista de aquí, de allá, del mundo, del cielo, del instante y del futuro y del pasado. Para los seres materialistas, ello no es más que una desgracia vista de este mundo: como ser pobre, caerse, ponerse en ridículo, etc.

For absolute souls, death is a timeless calamity, a calamity seen from here, from there, from the world, from heaven, from now and from the future and from the past. For materialist beings, it's nothing more than a calamity seen from this world: like being poor, falling down, making a fool of yourself, etc.

UNA nueva poética: transportar al poema la estética de Picasso. Es decir: no atender sino a las bellezas estrictamente poéticas, sin lógica ni coherencia, ni razón. Como cuando Picasso pinta a un hombre y, por razones de armonía de líneas o de colores, en vez de hacerle una nariz, hace en su lugar una caja o escalera o vaso o naranja.

A new poetics: carry over to the poem Picasso's esthetic. That is: attend to nothing but strictly poetic beauties, with neither logic nor coherence nor reason. As when Picasso paints a human figure and, for purposes of harmony of line or color, instead of giving it a nose, puts in its place a box or a ladder or a glass or an orange.

YO quiero que mi vida caiga por igual sobre todas y cada una de las cifras (44 kilos) de mi peso.

I want my life to fall equally on each and every unit (44 kilos) of my weight.

Mi metro mide dos metros; mi kilo pesa una tonelada.

My meter measures two meters; my kilo weighs a ton.

La risa por cosquillas y la risa por alegría moral. Rabelais.

TICKLISH laughter and morally joyous laughter. Rabelais.

El amor me libera en el sentido que *puedo* dejar de amar. La persona a quien amo debe dejarme la libertad de poder aborrecerla en cualquier momento.

LOVE liberates me insofar as I *am able* to leave off loving. The person I love must leave me the freedom to be able to hate her at any moment.

La aviación en el aire, en el agua y en el espíritu. Sus leyes en los tres casos son diversas. El espíritu vuela cuando pesa y se hunde más en sí mismo. Más grávido es un espíritu, más alto y más lejos vuela.

AVIATION in air, in water and in spirit. Its laws are different in all three cases. The spirit soars the more it weighs and sinks into itself. The heavier the spirit, the higher and farther it flies.

La mecánica es un medio o disciplina para realizar la vida, pero no es la vida misma. Esa debe llevarnos a la vida misma, que está en el juego de sentimientos o sea en la sensibilidad. Walt Whitman, Vallejo.

MECHANICS is a means or discipline for the realization of life, but not life itself. It ought to carry us to life itself, which is at play in feelings, or sensitivity. Walt Whitman, Vallejo.

Yo amo a las plantas por la raíz y no por la flor.

I love plants for the root, not for the flower.

LA naturaleza crea la eternidad de la substancia.
El arte crea la eternidad de la forma.

NATURE creates eternity of substance. Art creates eternity of form.

NADIE muere sino después de haber hecho alguna cosa interesante. Ése o aquél ha hecho algo interesante, puesto que ahora muere.

No one dies without having done some interesting thing. This one or that one has done something interesting, since he's now dying.

Las artes (pintura, poesía, etc.) no son sólo éstas. Artes son también comer, beber, caminar: todo acto es un arte. Resbalón hacia el dadaísmo.

THE arts (painting, poetry, etc.) are not just these. Eating, drinking, walking are also arts; every act is an art. The slippery slope toward dadaism.

SE copia una marca automovilístca y el copiador es enjuiciado y paga daños y perjuicios. Se copia un poema y no sucede nada. En Europa, se hace algo, pero es infinitamente pequeño e insignificante.

AN automobile trademark is copied and the copier is judged and pays fines and damages. A poem is copied and nothing happens. In Europe, something happens, but it's infinitely small and insignificant.

Escribí un verso en que hablaba de un adjetivo en el cual crecía la hierba. Unos años más tarde, en París, vi en una piedra del cementerio de Montparnasse un adjetivo con hierba. Profecía de la poesía.

I wrote a line where I spoke of grass growing out of an adjective. A few years later, in Paris, I saw on a stone in Montparnasse Cemetery an adjective growing grass. The prophecy of poetry.

Mi anarquía simple, mi gran dolor compuesto de alegrías.

My simple anarchy, my great pain composed of joys.

—Te debo 20 francos; préstame 5 y te quedaré debiendo 15. ¿Comprendes?

– I owe you 20 francs; lend me 5 and I'll only owe you 15. Get it?

VA a hacer caca y por esó se pone los anteojos.

He's going to take a shit and that's why he puts on his glasses.

VA al reservado y por eso se pone los lentes.

HE'S off to the private compartment, so he's putting his glasses on.

OYENDO a Beethoven, una mujer y un hombre lloran ante la grandeza de esa música. Y yo les digo: si son ustedes los que tienen en su corazón esta grandeza.

Listening to Beethoven, a woman and a man are crying faced with the greatness of that music. And I say to them: maybe it's you who have this greatness in your hearts.

Una estética nueva: poemas cortos, multiformes, sobre momentos evocativos o anticipaciones, como "L'Opérateur" en cinema de Vertof.

A new esthetic: short, multiform poems, on evocative moments or presentiments, like "L'Operateur" in Vertof's film.

¡CUIDADO con la substancia humana de la poesía!

CAREFUL with the human substance of poetry!

Si no ha de ser bonita la vida, que se lo coman todo.

If life's not going to be pretty, let them eat it all.

La incomprehensión de España sobre los escritores sudamericanos que, por miedo, no osaban ser indoamericanos, sino totalmente españoles. (Rubén Darío y otros).

Lorca en andaluz. ¿Por qué no tengo yo el derecho de ser peruano? ¿Para que me digan que no me comprenden en España? Y yo, un austriaco o un inglés, comprendemos los giros castizos de Lorca y Co.

Spain's incomprehension of South American writers who, out of fear, don't dare be Indoamerican, but instead utterly Spanish. (Rubén Darío and others.)

Lorca in Andalusian. Why don't I have the right to be Peruvian? So they can tell me they don't understand me in Spain? And I, an Austrian or an Englishman can understand the purebred turns of Lorca & Co.

Printed in Great Britain
by Amazon